Just Because

Where Another Point of View Makes a Better *You*!

Ferne Press

Written by Amber Housey • Illustrated by Denise Clemmensen

Just Because: Where Another Point of View Makes a Better You
Copyright © 2012 by Amber Housey
Illustrated by Denise Clemmensen
Printed in Canada

Illustrations created with watercolors.

Summary: Two families decide what they can do to help others.

Library of Congress Cataloging-in-Publication Data
Housey, Amber
Just Because: Where Another Point of View Makes a Better You/Amber Housey—First Edition
ISBN-13: 978-1-933916-90-3
1. Juvenile Fiction. 2. Charity. 3. Making a Difference. 4. Different Perspective. 5. Family. 6. Empathy and Compassion. 7. Donations/Community Service. 8. Values.
I. Housey, Amber II. Just Because: Where Another Point of View Makes a Better You
Library of Congress Control Number: 2011937375

FERNE PRESS

Ferne Press is an imprint of Nelson Publishing & Marketing
366 Welch Road, Northville, MI 48167
www.nelsonpublishingandmarketing.com
(248) 735-0418

To the devoted volunteers of Building Bridges Charity of Michigan for their dedication to "doing good things for kids."

To Carlos G., Norup Middle School, who called me his angel.

Thank you to my husband for his support and believing in me and to my three beautiful children for their love and excitement. Thank you to my Mom and Dad for their gifts of writing and creativity. Thank you to Michael D. Scott, a fellow author, Marilyn Stephan for publishing my first poem, and my students at Rogers Elementary who inspired these stories. Lastly, thank you to Marian Nelson and Kris Yankee at Nelson Publishing & Marketing for making my dream come true.

Today I woke and heard a noise
and wondered what it was.
I got right up and started down
and then I heard the buzz.

I paused a moment on the stair
and heard my mom and dad:
"To throw away is such a shame
for wasting is so sad."

Empty boxes on the floor
were scattered all around.
I wondered what they could be for;
a mystery I had found.

My sister climbed into a box
and asked what it was for.
"Come sit down," my mother said.
She got up from the floor.

Mother turned and said to us,
to Emily and me,
"We're cleaning and we're sorting out
everything we see."

Mom was cooking while she spoke,
"First we'll have a bite.
Here's some pancakes, sausage too."
She always does them right.

"We'll collect some clothes and toys
that we no longer need.
When we're done, we'll pack them up,
and I will take the lead."

"But Mom," we said, "we love them all,
every toy and shoe."
"We simply cannot give them up,
and give them up to who?"

"My dears, you see, we have so much,
more than so many.
We save a dollar, maybe ten
while others save a penny."

"We make a difference if we share
the items we don't use.
Give to some who are in need,
together we can choose."

We finished breakfast, got to work,
and looked at all our stuff.
As I looked, I realized,
that I have enough.

I sorted toys I didn't use,
like cars and balls and games.
It was hard to give them up,
especially my trains.

My sister sat there on the floor,
staring at her clothes.
"I like the pink. I like the blue.
I'll wear that if it snows."

She worked it out and made a pile
of clothes she didn't wear.
We took them down to show my mom
the ones we chose to share.

Mom reminded us again
what our purpose was.
Give to others who are in need
and do it just because.

"Can we really make a change?
We are so very small."
"If every person does their part,
we can conquer all."

We took the boxes to a place
with clothes stacked up for miles.
I saw a lady searching through
and I began to smile.

Her shoes were old with holes right through,
her clothes were not the best.
She searched and smiled when she found
my mom's pretty dress.

We learned we made a difference,
by what we did today,
for those with less but special, still,
in every single way.

Throughout the year, we like to share
and give to a cause.
We donate money and our time
and do it just because.

Let's look at the flip side.
Where seeing another point of view
makes a better you…

Today we woke and heard a noise,
I sat up in my bed.
We looked to where we heard the sound.
"I'm scared," my sister said.

Our closet door began to move.
Just what could it be?
Then I saw her stepping out,
"Morning," she said to me.

"Why are you in there," I asked,
"looking at my clothes?"
"I want to see what you need
and also see what goes."

My sister jumped out of bed.
and climbed into a box.
She asked my mom, "What's this for?"
while playing with my socks.

My dad smiled and picked her up;
he put her on the bed.
"We're going to the thrifty store,
to buy some things," he said.

Mom took the box and said to us,
"Let's go have a bite.
We'll have some toast and some juice.
Please turn off the light."

"Some socks, some shoes, and other clothes,
we'll buy what we need.
We'll go today and bring them home.
and I will take the lead."

"Mom," we said, "we need some clothes,
but have no money to buy."
"We get some help from friendly folks."
And then she gave a sigh.

"My dears, you see, we have so little,
less than so many.
Some save a dollar, maybe ten.
We must save our pennies.

"But we can make a difference.
Others have needs too.
To throw away what can be used
is a wasteful thing to do."

We finished breakfast and got a pen
and wrote down all we need.
She said our wants will have to wait;
We have to watch our greed.

"There are toys I'd like to have,
like a car or ball or game.
But there is other stuff we need,
I want them just the same."

My sister sat there on the floor,
playing with a toy
that someone else had given away,
from another girl or boy.

After we gathered a bunch of items
that we chose to share.
We boxed them up to give away
and set them by the stairs.

Mom continued to explain
what the purpose was;
to give to others who are in need
and do it just because.

"Can we really make a change?
We are so very small."
"If every person does their part,
we can conquer all."

Off we traveled to the place
where clothes are piled high.
I love to look around and choose
the things I hope we buy.

Our shoes are old with holes right through,
our clothes are not the best.
We searched and found some things we like.
My mother found a dress.

Today we learned that what we do,
be it big or small,
others still have less than us.
We answer to the call.

When we can, we volunteer,
or donate to a cause.
We've learned to help and give and share,
and do it just because.

Take a look at another's view,
see a perspective that may be new.
Walk in someone else's shoes,
in their footprints if you choose.
Try to see from where they come,
use your feelings, we all have some.
They help us feel for those in need,
for those who hurt and those who bleed.
They make us smile when good is done,
they make us laugh when something's fun.
Hop on board and join the ride,
and take a look at The Flip Side.

In this book, the author and illustrator added
characters and things related to future
Flip Side Stories. Can you find them?

Mango (7 places)

Victor (1 place)

mirror (2 places)

rope (3 places)

army boots (2 places)

robot (4 places)

Did you notice the baby in the second family
always reaching for the teddy bear?

bear (10 places)   **lion (7 places)**

-where seeing another point of view makes a better you.

Just Because was inspired by the work I have done with Building Bridges, a charity my husband founded. I lead a gifting program that supports families in need during the holidays. I hope to inspire children and their families to find ways to help those in need in their communities by volunteering their time or donating new and used items. This story shares two perspectives or points of view that show the impact of giving to those who are less fortunate and do it just because. This also encourages empathy and compassion for others.

 A portion of the proceeds from this book will benefit Building Bridges Charity of Michigan.

 **www.buildingbridgescharity.org**

ABOUT THE AUTHOR

Amber is happily married and a mother of three beautiful children (and two dogs, Mango and Hershey). She lives in Troy, Michigan. Amber taught preschool in Huntington Woods and then taught first and second grade in Berkley. She loves to inspire children to love learning and be creative. Amber holds degrees in Liberal Arts, Early Childhood, Elementary Education, and a Masters in the Art in Teaching. She loves drawing, photography, technology, kickboxing, volunteering, and of course, writing stories. For more information about Amber, please visit her website at **www.theflipsidestories.com.**

ABOUT THE ILLUSTRATOR

Denise has been an artist from the moment she first tore open a box of crayons. Her parents, being wise, bought the budding young artist a drawing table, hoping to somehow redirect her creativity away from any tangible surfaces…siblings included. Denise grew up in the San Fernando Valley, a suburb of Los Angeles, where her love of art grew from kindergarten through college. She has been a graphic artist, muralist, librarian, singer-songwriter, and stay-at-home mom. She still lives in "the Valley" with her husband of thirty years and her two grown children. Besides her family, Denise has always had a love affair with children's literature.